Other books by the author available
from Scholastic Book Services . . .

- **THE BOATNIKS**
- **THE LOVE BUG**
- **MONKEYS, GO HOME!**
  dic-tion-ar-y skilz
  **MAN IN A GREEN BERET AND
  OTHER MEDAL OF HONOR
  WINNERS**

- Adapted from the Walt Disney
  motion pictures

Walt Disney Productions...

RIDES AGAIN

Adapted by MEL CEBULASH from
the Walt Disney motion picture

SCHOLASTIC BOOK SERVICES

NEW YORK•TORONTO•LONDON•AUCKLAND•SYDNEY•TOKYO

ISBN: 0-590-08821-1

18 17 16 15 14 13 12 11 10 9 8   0 1 2 3 4 5/8

CAST OF CHARACTERS
for
HERBIE RIDES AGAIN

	Played by
Mrs. Steinmetz	Helen Hayes
Willoughby Whitfield	Ken Berry
Nicole	Stefanie Powers
Mr. Judson	John McIntire
Alonzo Hawk	Keenan Wynn
Chauffeur	Ivor Barry
Lawyers	Dan Tobin and
	Raymond Bailey
Taxi Driver	Vito Scotti
Secretary	Elaine Devry
Loostgarten	Chuck McCann
Traffic Commissioner	Richard X. Slattery
Sir Lancelot	Hank Jones
Red Knight	Rod McCary

and

HERBIE

ONE

The TV cameras rolled and the gold curtain
lifted, revealing a model of a huge 130-story skyscraper.

"That's it, ladies and gentlemen," the master
of ceremonies announced over the applause of
San Francisco's civic leaders. "Hawk Plaza, the
world's highest office building! In just a few
hours, Hawk Enterprises will break ground on
this incredible project."

The M.C. paused, allowing the city's leaders
to step forward for a closer view of the model.
Then he continued, "How did it happen, you
ask? I give you now the man who made it all pos-
sible. A man who is both proud and humble — a

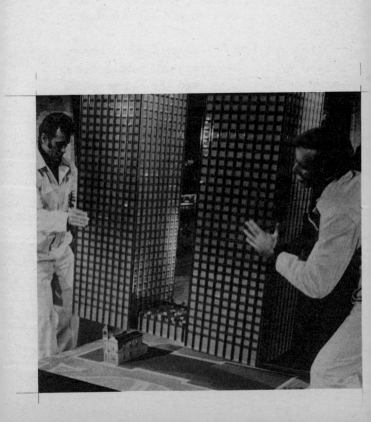

sophisticated dynamo who is still a farm boy at heart. I give you Alonzo Hawk — himself!"

A door in the rear of the room opened and through it stepped Alonzo Hawk. Generous applause greeted him, and the silver in his beard seemed to glitter with approval. Then he raised his hand and his audience responded with silence. "Thank you, friends," he said, dabbing gently at one eye. "My heart is too filled to speak. You see, you've brought a tear to this flinty old eye. All I can say is thank you. Thank you for allowing me to share a moment of your precious time!"

Again the leaders applauded, while waiters rushed to refill their champagne glasses. For a slight moment, Hawk eyed the festive scene. Then he leaned over to the master of ceremonies and whispered, "Get these deadheads out of here! Don't they have anything to do but stand around here and guzzle my booze?"

Hawk turned quickly and went off into his office. The phone was ringing. Picking it up, he said, "Yeah?"

"This is Barnsdorf," the caller said. "I'm down at the site with some of my boys. When are you going to be ready for us to dig?"

"I'm ready now!" Hawk screamed into the

Two men from Hawk Enterprises lift model of world's highest office building to reveal hold-out—a small antique firehouse!

3

phone. "Go ahead and dig. What are you waiting for?"

At the other end, Barnsdorf glanced from his construction trailer to a firehouse sitting solidly amid the remains of many other buildings. "Oh come on, Hawk!" Barnsdorf answered. "The site isn't cleared yet. You know very well that the firehouse is still there."

"What's that?" Hawk questioned. "I thought we got rid of that crummy little firehouse months ago. Well, you just sit tight, Barnsdorf. I'll get back to you."

Hawk slammed down the phone. Then he buzzed for his secretary on the intercom. "Get all those miserable lawyers in here, and fast!" he said.

Minutes later, Hawk's lawyers meekly entered the office, nervously lined up in front of him.

"There's been one tiny holdup, Mr. Hawk," one lawyer explained nervously. "We couldn't get old lady Steinmetz to sign the final papers."

"One miserable little old lady," Hawk sneered, "and she makes monkeys out of the most overpaid lawyers in the country! Come on, boys. I expect action from you, and I'm going to get it or else!"

"For some reason, Mrs. Steinmetz doesn't seem to trust us," another lawyer said.

Hawk glanced at the anxious faces of his lawyers. "Of course not!" he roared. "Ever look at yourselves? Your own mothers wouldn't trust you! What we need is someone nauseatingly innocent, stomach-turningly helpful, and so incredibly dumb that anyone would trust him!"

Before any of the lawyers could answer, Hawk's intercom sounded. Hawk's secretary had just finished talking with young Willoughby Whitfield and had asked him to have a seat. Whitfield, a pleasant-looking man, seated himself on the edge of a chair. On his lap he held a plaque — an award for Alonzo Hawk.

"Mr. Willoughby Whitfield to see you," Hawk's secretary announced. "He says he's your nephew."

"Whoever he is, throw him out!" Hawk's voice roared through the intercom. "And don't bother me again!"

Hawk's secretary glanced up at Willoughby, wondering how she was going to give him the message, but he had heard it. Smiling weakly, he got up and started for the door. Then the intercom sounded, and the secretary answered it.

"Wait a minute!" Hawk said. "Is that that dumb-looking kid of my sister's from somewhere back East? Just starting law school — or something?"

Glancing at Willoughby, who had stopped

and turned her way, the secretary answered, "He's just *finished* law school, sir. He says he's a full-fledged lawyer."

"A full-fledged lawyer!" Hawk repeated with delight in his voice. "Well, send him in. Send him right in!"

As Willoughby stumbled through the door, Hawk smiled and said to his chief lawyer, "He's beautiful! Perfectly beautiful!"

Bewildered by the sudden change of events, Willoughby stepped forward and handed the plaque to Hawk. "Uncle?" he said, clearing his throat. "Uncle Alonzo, I hereby present you with the Furze Law College 'Humanitarian of the Year' award."

Hawk looked over the plaque. "Well, Humanitarian of the Year!" he said, suspiciously. "Look, kiddo, I know these award committees sometimes give Humanitarian Awards to a lot of strange ducks, but why *me*?"

Willoughby coughed. Then he said, "I was the Award Committee."

"Oh, I get it," Hawk said smiling. "You put the fix in. You figured to take care of your Uncle Alonzo. You're a smart boy. If there's one thing I admire, it's someone who knows how to use juice properly."

"Juice?" Willoughby asked, a puzzled look on his face.

6

"Juice!" Hawk repeated. "How to use muscle! How to use influence! Bend things his own way!"

"Oh no, it wasn't done dishonestly," Willoughby corrected. "I thought it over and thought it over, but I couldn't think of anyone more deserving than you, Uncle Alonzo."

"How come?" Hawk asked.

Willoughby stood at attention. "From the day I was born," he said, "Mother never tired of telling me what a great man her brother was — getting rid of dirty old buildings — building shiny new ones — sending us fruit at Christmas. You were her idol, and you *are* my idol!"

Hawk glanced at his lawyers. Their mouths were hanging open. They had heard the words, but they still couldn't believe. "You clowns get out of here," Hawk ordered. "I want to have a nice talk with my favorite nephew!"

The lawyers scurried off, and Hawk motioned Willoughby into a chair. Then he gave the young man a huge cigar and lit it for him.

"I'm old and crusty and battle-worn," Hawk told his nephew. "But when I look into your eyes and see the shining light of idealism aglow there, I'm young again and ready for the battle."

"Battle?" Willoughby coughed on his cigar.

"Yes, my boy, battle," Hawk said. "Things have never been easy for us idealists. But what

7

I'm going to do now is give you the chance to put your idealism into play on your very first job."

Hawk paused, surprised and delighted at his own words. Then he started to pace the floor. "Picture, if you will, a tough little old lady, living in a rundown, rat-infested firehouse, standing right in the way of our latest civic benefaction," he said. "Now your average city builder might find it in his heart to be vengeful toward that little old lady. He might say she feeds on the miseries of the poor in that forsaken neighborhood, that she rolls drunks, that she teaches little children to steal and bring her most of the money. But would Alonzo Hawk, Humanitarian of the Year, stoop to such tactics?"

"Of course not, Uncle!" Willoughby interrupted.

"Of course not," Hawk continued. "Alonzo Hawk would do everything in his power to help that tough no-good little old lady. He would give her a large sum of money for her worthless old property. Then he would provide — at a special price for her only — a lifetime lease in Eternity Towers, that beautiful new apartment home for helpless old people like herself. With a gymnasium, a sauna bath, and old Clark Gable movies! A beauty parlor! A hobby center! And instead of cooking her heart out over a hot stove, she would have automatic machines in every hall to thrill her with everything from pizza to

8

hot chili! Willoughby, wouldn't it make your whole being happy to be part of all that?"

Willoughby jumped up. "When can I start, Uncle?" He sounded inspired.

Smiling to himself, Hawk reached for a piece of paper on his desk. "Here's the address," he told Willoughby. "Get moving, my boy. Get moving!"

TWO

The following morning, Willoughby called a taxicab, directing the driver to the address on the slip of paper his uncle had given him. Willoughby liked what he saw of San Francisco through the cab window. He guessed many of the new buildings were built by his uncle, and he was glad that he was being given a chance to help.

At the end of a short trip, the cab slowed to a stop. Willoughby saw a number of vacant lots and some rubble. He also saw the large sign that read "Hawk Plaza to be built here." On the sign was a picture of his uncle's new building. A similar sign was on a wall next to the one remaining building — a firehouse.

"It's going to be a lovely building," Willoughby thought, handing his fare to the driver.

Then he said, "Isn't it breathtaking?"

"Yeah," the driver answered sadly. "It's a mess all right. That guy Hawk ought to be hung."

The cab moved off, leaving Willoughby slightly puzzled by the driver's response. But he didn't have time to worry about it. He had a mission to accomplish. Briskly he stepped up to the door of the firehouse and rang the bell. Then he stepped out into the street to look over the building.

While he was looking, the front wheel of the little car he was standing by rolled onto his foot. Just then a cheerful-looking little woman opened the door of the firehouse. Trying to pull his foot loose, Willoughby said politely, "Good morning, Mrs. Steinmetz. My name is Willoughby Whitfield. I'd like to discuss a little business with you."

"Well, come in, won't you?" Mrs. Steinmetz was very friendly.

"I can't," Willoughby answered, still struggling by the little car. "This car has run over my foot."

Mrs. Steinmetz hurried over to Willoughby's side. She was carrying a teapot, and she handed it to Willoughby.

"Guess somebody forgot to set the brake or

11

something," Willoughby told her.

"Herbie, aren't you ashamed!" Mrs. Steinmetz said to the little car. "Now you get off Mr. Whitfield's foot this instant!"

Then she gave the little car a slight push, and it rolled off Willoughby's foot.

A look of surprise came over Willoughby's face. He couldn't understand how the little old woman could push a car so easily. She didn't appear to be very strong.

"Herbie is always trying to protect me," Mrs. Steinmetz said, "but I'm perfectly capable of taking care of myself, you know."

"Herbie?" said Willoughby, wondering if his uncle had forgotten to tell him there was something wrong with Mrs. Steinmetz's mind.

Mrs. Steinmetz took the teapot back from Willoughby. Then she said, "Come right in, young man. I was just going to make myself a nice cup of tea, and you must have one with me."

Willoughby followed the little woman into the firehouse. There she turned to him and said, secretively, "Of course I have to humor Herbie. He's a little touchy. He used to be a famous racing car, but his driver went off to Europe to drive foreign cars. You can understand that."

"Oh, sure," Willoughby said with an even more puzzled look on his face. "But, now,

Mrs. Steinmetz, let's get down to business. People have been worrying about your living in this old firetrap."

"Firehouse, young man!" Mrs. Steinmetz corrected. "Not firetrap!"

Willoughby began to answer, but a blast of music interrupted him. He looked around and saw that the music was coming from an ancient orchestrion and its colored lights were flashing.

"Stop it!" Mrs. Steinmetz told the orchestrion. She spoke severely, "You're being downright rude."

The music stopped, and the orchestrion's lights snapped off. Then Mrs. Steinmetz giggled slightly and said, "Do you know what he was playing, Mr. Whitfield? 'Do Not Trust Him, Gentle Maiden.' Nothing personal, I imagine. He's a friend of Herbie's, of course."

Willoughby stared blankly at the little old woman. "Herbie's friend?" he said.

Mrs. Steinmetz motioned Willoughby to follow her to a side door. Through the door, they could see a battered old cable car filled with pots of flowers. "This is 'Old 22,'" Mrs. Steinmetz said. "Another friend of Herbie's. He used to be on the old Clay Street line. Herbie found him in a vacant lot. Someone had been using him as a chicken house, but he's much happier here, of course."

13

Mrs. Steinmetz went back to her tea-making and Willoughby followed, anxious to get to the job his uncle had given him.

"I can quite understand that you may have some emotional attachment to this rickety old building," Willoughby began.

But Mrs. Steinmetz interrupted him. "Indeed I do," she said. "Do you know that I was married here to my late husband, Captain Steinmetz of the San Francisco Fire Department, one of the heroes of the Great Fire?"

"We understand, Mrs. Steinmetz, but Mr. Hawk does want to — "

Again Mrs. Steinmetz interrupted. "Don't tell me you're from Alonzo Hawk?" she said sharply. "And you have such a nice face! Not at all like those roughnecks he usually sends around!"

"Here!" Willoughby responded. "Just look at the size of this check."

"Oh, I don't know anything about money," the little old woman said. "My nephew, Tennessee Steinmetz, usually takes care of me. He used to live here, but he had to rush to Tibet because his guru is sick."

"Guru?" Willoughby repeated. "What's a guru?"

"His teacher, of course. My nephew is a student of Oriental philosophy. That's how he found things have an inner life — like wind and

14

rain and traffic lights and can openers and flowers and little cars. That's how Tennessee and Herbie became the best of friends."

Willoughby wished he could get back to the subject. "Mrs. Steinmetz," he said, "this sum of money could take care of you the rest of your life."

Mrs. Steinmetz smiled proudly. "But I didn't have to study Oriental philosophy as Tennessee did," she said. "I could talk to Herbie right away. I suppose it's in the blood."

Outside, a small airport bus had stopped in front of the firehouse. A stewardess got out. Waving to the bus as it pulled away, she took out her keys and moved to the firehouse door. As she entered, she heard someone say the name "Hawk," and then she quietly closed the door.

Willoughby had taken a piece of paper from his pocket. "I have an agreement here," he said. "If you would just glance at it, you would understand its many advantages."

Mrs. Steinmetz looked at Willoughby and saw the stewardess standing behind him. "Oh, Nicole!" she said. "I want you to meet a gentleman from Mr. Hawk's."

Willoughby turned and smiled at the attractive young woman.

"How do you do," Nicole said, and at the same time, she hit Willoughby with a hard, roundhouse right to the chin.

Willoughby fell to the floor, out cold. "Bothering us again, are they?" Nicole said sadly.

Mrs. Steinmetz dropped to Willoughby's side and tried to bring him back to consciousness. "Oh, poor Mr. Whitfield," she said. "Such a nice young man!"

Seconds later, Willoughby opened his eyes slightly, and Mrs. Steinmetz said, "Are you all right, Mr. Whitfield?"

"What was that?" Willoughby asked, still trying to clear his head.

"Nicole Harris. A very brave young lady. She works for the airline people. Last week she knocked out a hijacker with a bottle of wine."

Nicole came over and helped Willoughby to his feet. "Now split!" she told him. "If you or any more of Hawk's stooges come around here again, you'll get worse than that!"

"Please stop, Nicole," Mrs. Steinmetz said. "Mr. Whitfield and I were having a nice conversation."

"I'll bet," Nicole said, "but it's time for your nap now."

"Oh, very well," Mrs. Steinmetz said, starting upstairs for her room. "Good-bye, Mr. Whitfield. Perhaps I'll see you when I come down."

Willoughby looked over at Nicole. She was in

Nicole Harris, properly appraising his nefarious intentions, leads with right to Willoughby Whitfield's jaw!

no mood to be friendly. She thumbed him toward the front door and said, "Blow!"

"Have a heart, miss," Willoughby begged. "This is my first assignment. I can't afford to fail!"

Nicole didn't answer, but Willoughby could read her mind, especially when he saw her reaching for a bottle on the table.

"I'll go! I'll go!" he said, and stumbled out the front door, Nicole close behind.

In the fresh air again, Willoughby picked up more courage. He turned to Nicole and said, "You seem like a sensible person. You must know that living alone in this crummy neighborhood is no place for an elderly woman!"

"Who says she's alone?" Nicole answered. "She's got me, and she's got Herbie too."

"That's another thing. A sure sign she's coming apart. Those fantasies of old age. Particularly that goofy story about this little car," he said, glancing at the VW.

"You think it's goofy?"

"Don't you?" he asked.

Nicole thought for a moment. Then she said, "How'd you like to take a ride in this little car?"

Willoughby smiled. "I thought you didn't like me," he said.

"Well, I'd like to take you for a ride in Herbie. I'd like that a lot."

"Fine," Willoughby said. "That's very nice of you."

"I'll be ready in a minute," Nicole said. Then she turned and went back into the firehouse.

While he was waiting, Willoughby looked over the little VW. He couldn't believe the way the old lady and Nicole had spoken about it. Without thinking, he kicked one of its rear tires and turned away.

Herbie responded with an angry beep of his horn. The noise startled Willoughby, but he still wasn't ready to accept Herbie as a thinking creature. There had to be a mechanical explanation for the horn's blowing by itself.

When Nicole returned, he noticed that she had changed to another, more attractive dress. He smiled and quickly opened the car door for her.

Nicole quickly fastened her seat belt and started the car, and Willoughby got in beside her. "Your seat belt, please," Nicole said to him. "Herbie is fussy about seat belts."

Willoughby couldn't believe all the Herbie talk, but humoring her, he fastened his belt. Then the car began moving slowly down the street.

"Come on, Herb," Nicole said. "Let's get on with it!"

"Miss Harris," Willoughby said, "you're obviously an intelligent young woman. Why do you pretend to talk to this little car like that?"

Nicole didn't answer. "Don't listen to him, Herb," she said. "Just do your thing!"

"I can understand your Mrs. Steinmetz thinking of this car as a person," Willoughby said. "Old age has its problems. It only proves she needs Mr. Hawk's help."

"Give it to him, Herb!" Nicole urged, but the car continued to move slowly. Then she said angrily, "Stubborn little bucket of bolts! Always have to do everything your own way, don't you?"

"Let's stop kidding ourselves," Willoughby said. "This is just an ordinary little car. It's like a million other ordinary rather unattractive little cars."

UNATTRACTIVE! Herbie had heard enough! He gunned his motor! He reared up on his back wheels! Then with a sudden jolt, he began to race down the street like a streak of lightning!

Willoughby and Nicole were taken by surprise. They both hung on as best they could, while the little car careered through the streets.

UNATTRACTIVE! Well, Herbie has heard enough! He goes into his bucking act.

THREE

Willoughby didn't think any VW could go as fast as he was riding. But he was sure it wasn't racing by itself, and he was going to hang on until Nicole stopped her little joke.

"I don't think you should have said that about Herbie," Nicole said. "He's sensitive about his appearance."

"OK," Willoughby said. "You've had your laugh. But I think you ought to stop now."

"You'll never get Herbie to stop unless you tell him you're sorry."

Willoughby frowned. "Miss Harris," he said, "the thing that upsets me most about this whole thing is your trying to maintain the story about this bottle-nosed car being able to think."

Again Herbie reacted to an adverse remark about his appearance. He revved up and headed right for the cars crossing a crowded intersection. There was no doubt that Herbie was going through the red light on the corner. Willoughby and Nicole ducked behind the little car's dashboard and waited for the crash. But somehow Herbie managed to avoid all the cars and get through intact.

With some hesitation, Willoughby and Nicole lifted themselves back into a sitting position. Then Nicole said, "If you don't care about your life, I care about mine. Now tell Herbie you're sorry."

Still doubtful, Willoughby gritted his teeth and spoke, "All right. I'm sorry, Herbie."

Herbie slowed down and then came to a quick stop. "What do you think now?" Nicole asked.

"I think *you* are a very skillful driver," Willoughby answered. "But I don't know if I'd like to have you drive me again."

Looking at Willoughby, Nicole said, "You still think it's a trick. Well, get out and come around to this side and drive. You need another lesson from Herbie."

While Nicole slid across the seat, Willoughby walked around the little car and got in on the driver's side. Then he started the VW. It behaved normally, and Willoughby grinned at Nicole. She didn't see his grin. She was staring ahead grimly.

"You see?" Willoughby told her. "As I was saying, this car is just your ordinary, rather stupid-looking little car."

He'd done it again! Herbie roared! Then he wheeled and rocketed straight ahead down the highway!

Willoughby had lost control. He was terrified. He tried the brake. He tried the gearshift. He tried the emergency brake. But Herbie wasn't having it. He refused to stop! Not for Willoughby!

"What do I do now?" Willoughby screamed.

"Too late!" Nicole said wearily. "You're on your own! I just hope Herb hasn't lost his sense of humor!"

Herbie turned onto a dirt raceway used by hot rod drivers. As he went under a banner stretched across the road, Willoughby read it to himself. "Ye Chickene Tournament! Jousting Today 11 A.M. — Big Prizes."

"What's it up to now?" Willoughby asked meekly.

"Don't know. It's hard to figure Herbie sometimes."

Herbie moved into an area with a lot of beat-up old cars in it. They were being worked on by young people wearing medieval clothes. Everywhere Willoughby looked he could see banners and medieval style flags. He tried the door of the little VW, but Herbie wasn't letting him out.

"Hear ye! Hear ye!" a field announcer's voice commanded. "The most gallant and chivalrous contestants for Joust Number Six will take their positions at opposite ends of the lists! Repeat! Contestants for Joust Number Six, take your places! We wish you well, brave knights!"

As Willoughby and Nicole watched, a single car lined up at the north end and another at the south end of the dirt track.

"There is the undefeated champion," the announcer said, and the young people in the stands cheered for a young man wearing a red plumed helmet in the car at the north end. "It's the Red Knight. At the south end, you see his stouthearted opponent, Sir Lancelot!"

"I don't know what Herbie's up to," Nicole whispered, "but I hope it isn't what I think it is."

Willoughby didn't respond. A trumpet had sounded, and the joust was beginning.

With his engine roaring, the Red Knight took off down the strip. Quickly, the two cars came almost face-to-face. But just as they were about to crash, Sir Lancelot spun his wheel, swerving out of the red car's way.

The crowd in the grandstand made a series of rooster noises, and a huge card with the word "chicken" on it was raised for Sir Lancelot.

"That seems dangerous to me," Willoughby said. Then he noticed some teenagers were tapping Herbie's headlights. "Hey! What are you doing?" he called to them.

"I think I'll split," Nicole said, opening the car door and getting out.

"Good idea!" Willoughby said. Then he tried to open his door. It wouldn't open. He quickly slid across the seat toward the door Nicole had left open, but it slammed shut in his face.

As Willoughby beat on the windows, trying to get out, the little car moved forward, and Nicole waved to its trapped passenger.

"I think Herb plans to make a believer out of you!" Nicole called.

"Good ladies, fine gentlemen — our lion-hearted contestants are preparing the seventh joust of the afternoon!" the announcer said. "At the north end, your favorite and mine, the Red Knight! And I don't have a name for the new challenger. But the name doesn't matter. No one lasts long against the Red Knight!"

Willoughby didn't need to know the name of the new challenger — he was sitting in it! The new challenger was Herbie!

"Let the joust begin," the announcer said, and the trumpet blew.

"That seems dangerous to me," Willoughby exclaims as Herbie prances about. Nicole grabs his arm for comfort.

The Red Knight and Herbie quickly started for each other from the opposite ends of the track. "Herbie, stop!" Willoughby screamed. "I believe! Honest, I do!"

Charging forward at top speed, the Red Knight bore a smile of confidence. He had defeated many other contestants, and he certainly didn't fear a little VW.

Willoughby was charging forward too, but he was hiding behind the dash and praying that Herbie would stop or turn around or do something else.

As the two cars came closer, the Red Knight's smile disappeared. It looked as if the little VW wasn't going to chicken out. Fear replaced confidence in the Red Knight's eyes.

In seconds, the cars were almost face to face. The Red Knight knew it was all over for him. He swung his wheel wildly, and the little VW caught him in the rear. He spun out on the sidelines and crashed. Cries of "chicken" spilled out of the grandstand, and the Red Knight saw the chicken banner being flashed at him.

Willoughby almost had himself together when Herbie stopped at the judges' stand. The judges and a blonde woman, "The Queen of Beauty," approached the little car. After taking a wreath of laurel from her head and placing it on Willoughby's head, the blonde woman kissed him.

"My brave champion!" she said. "You have

won me! Take me to your kingdom! Then a judge handed Willoughby a bag of coins and said, "You win the bread, man! Three dollars!"

Before Willoughby could respond, Herbie backed away right to the spot where Nicole was waiting and opened his door for her to get in. Willoughby slid over, allowing her to take the driver's seat.

Feeling victorious, Nicole said, "Well, has Herbie convinced you now?"

"I don't know," Willoughby said in honest confusion. "I'm a little mixed up, but I'm beginning to think I owe you an apology."

"Forget it," Nicole answered. "I can't stand men who apologize."

"Well, then let me take you to lunch," Willoughby suggested.

"That's OK."

"But not in this car," Willoughby said, opening his door.

Before he could move, the door slammed shut and locked. Then Herbie started off down the road.

Nicole leaned back in her seat, smiled, and said, "It seems to be out of our hands."

FOUR

Herbie must have had romance in mind. He took them to a lovely restaurant on picturesque Fisherman's Wharf in San Francisco.

Nicole and Willoughby were seated at a table on the Wharf, overlooking some fishing boats moored in the waters below. They each ordered lobster, and after the waiter had tied paper bibs around their necks, they began to talk.

"I used to live in a little apartment opposite the firehouse," Nicole explained. "It was old and I loved it. Then Hawk came along to tear the place down and threw me out."

The mention of Hawk unnerved Willoughby. Sooner or later, he was going to have to tell Nicole about his relationship to Alonzo Hawk. Deciding upon later, he said, "I'm sure he didn't mean it personally."

"Well, there I was, out in the street," Nicole continued. "So now you know why I go ape when I hear the name Hawk. Oh, and by the way, how is your jaw?"

"All right, I guess," Willoughby said, moving his jaw from side to side with his hand, wincing as he did it.

"I'm sorry," Nicole said. "But how did I know it was your first assignment for Hawk. Naturally, you couldn't know what a no-good he is."

Willoughby wanted to say something, to tell her about his uncle, but she went on. "Mrs. Steinmetz took me in, until I could find some other place," she said. "She's a great old lady. Then when I found what Hawk was up to, I decided to stay on to protect her. I wasn't about to let rats from Alonzo Hawk talk her out of her home."

"Miss Harris, I don't think you're being quite fair," Willoughby said, defensively.

"Fair?" Nicole repeated. "To Alonzo Hawk? Don't tell me that he's conned you the way he's conned everyone else in town?"

"No, but I have something to tell you."

"Don't tell me anything," Nicole answered. "Let me tell you. He put a parking garage on the lot where the DiMaggio brothers learned to play baseball. His factories are polluting all the fish

31

in the bay. His skyscraper throws a cold gray shadow over the children's playground all day long. He's moved thirty Chinese families off Grant Avenue to make room for his buildings."

Willoughby couldn't bear hearing any more about Alonzo Hawk. "Miss Harris," he pleaded, "I can't believe Uncle Alonzo would do things like that. I really can't."

In just seconds, the impact of Willoughby's words had Nicole boiling. "*Uncle!*" she screamed. "He's your *uncle*?"

"Yes," Willoughby said, relieved his secret was out. "That's why I happen to know Uncle Alonzo has a heart of gold. He's one of the finest." It was bad timing for Willoughby.

"You rotten spy!" Nicole screamed just as the waiter appeared with two gigantic broiled lobsters. Grabbing one of the lobsters, Nicole swung it into Willoughby's face. The impact sent him toppling over and through the railing into the waters of the little harbor. Nicole slammed the lobster back into the waiter's plate, got up, and rushed out of the restaurant.

In the meantime, Willoughby was being helped onto the deck of a small boat by a fisherman. Neither of them noticed the waiter who, deciding it was silly to take the damaged lobster

Grabbing gigantic boiled lobster, Nicole angrily flings it at Willoughby.

back to the kitchen, tossed it over his shoulder into the harbor.

The tossed lobster hit Willoughby, and he toppled back into the water, taking the fisherman with him.

Nicole missed Willoughby's second spill into the water. She was in Herbie on her way back to the firehouse, annoyed with herself for having been so friendly to Alonzo Hawk's nephew.

By night, Nicole had calmed down. She had discussed the matter with Mrs. Steinmetz, and the two women were getting ready to go to sleep. Mrs. Steinmetz was already in bed when Nicole entered her room with a glass of milk. "Here's your warm milk, Grandma," Nicole said. "Now you drink it. You know how good it is for you."

Taking the milk, Mrs. Steinmetz said, "I still don't understand why you hit him with a broiled lobster."

Nicole sat down on the bed. "I didn't plan it that way," she explained. "I really wish I could stop doing things like that. In fact, I really kind of like Willoughby."

"I'm glad you do, dear. After all, brilliant eligible lawyers don't grow on trees."

Nicole looked at Mrs. Steinmetz. Then she smiled and said, "Grandma, what's this leading up to?"

"Well, I thought perhaps you could talk

things over with this nice Mr. Whitfield. You two might be able to get together."

"Good try, Grandma," Nicole said sincerely. "But if I want a young man, I'll get him my own way."

"I suppose so, dear," Mrs. Steinmetz said. "I suppose so."

Rising and kissing Mrs. Steinmetz on the forehead, Nicole said, "Right! Now stop hatching plots, close those bright little eyes, and go to sleep."

Nicole started to leave. "Nonsense!" Mrs. Steinmetz called after her. "A girl needs all the help she can get! Good night, dear."

"Good night," Nicole said. Then she slid down the fireman's brass sliding pole to her room.

FIVE

After a night of tossing, turning, and thinking, Willoughby had come to some important decisions. He was leaving San Francisco. His uncle was as bad as Nicole said he was, and he wasn't going to do any dirty work for Alonzo Hawk.

He was packed and ready to go. He stood before the mirror in his room, practicing his farewell speech to his uncle and applying makeup to the black eyes Nicole had given him.

"Uncle Alonzo," he said to the mirror, "I dropped by to talk with you man to man. So I could look you squarely in the eye.

"I'm wearing makeup because of the black eyes. A girl hit me with a broiled lobster the moment I mentioned your name.

"This same wonderful clear-sighted girl was able to show me what kind of person you really are. Well, I do not hold with your scheme of cheating Mrs. Steinmetz out of her home so you can build your concrete anthill on the spot where she has known so much happiness. I think you are despicable, greedy, grasping, and wholly without principle or pity. I also believe you are not a nice person.

"If you write my mother — who is also your sister Freida — please do not tell her I wear makeup as a general rule.

"I am going back to Missouri now, so you may no longer use me as a cat's-paw. I bid you farewell more in sorrow than in anger. Please do not send us any more fruit for Christmas. Good-bye, Uncle."

Willoughby stepped away from the mirror and picked up his bag. He was pleased with his speech. First, he'd stop at the firehouse. Then he'd get to his uncle. Just before he left, he turned to the mirror again and said, "No, Uncle. Begging won't help!"

When Willoughby reached the firehouse, he talked to Herbie, explaining that he had no hard feelings. Then he realized the firehouse door was open and Mrs. Steinmetz, dressed to go out, was watching him.

"I'm glad you and Herbie decided to make up," she said, shutting the door behind her.

"I'm just off for my morning walk. Why don't you come with me and we can have a nice chat."

"I'm afraid I only came to say good-bye," Willoughby said sadly. "I'm going home to Hawk City, Missiouri."

"Oh what a pity," Mrs. Steinmetz said. "Nicole was so looking forward to seeing you again. She's a wonderful girl — even though you don't seem to agree with her."

"I do agree with her now," Willoughby corrected. "As a matter of fact, I'm going straight to my uncle and tell him exactly what I think of him. I know he's an important man, but it's time he heard the truth."

"Nicole will be thrilled to hear that. Everyone's so afraid of Mr. Hawk. Please stay until Nicole comes back. Then you can tell her."

Willoughby shuddered at the thought. "To be honest," he said, "I'm more afraid of her than I am of my uncle."

"Nonsense!" Mrs. Steinmetz said. "Nicole's just a high-spirited young lady."

"That's for sure!" Willoughby agreed. "But for some reason or other, I'm always getting hurt when she's around. Good-bye, Mrs. Steinmetz, and don't weaken about the firehouse."

"Don't worry, young man," Mrs. Steinmetz said, shaking his hand.

Then the little old woman watched Willoughby go. "What a fine young man, Herbie," she said to the VW. "Such a pity that he and Nicole couldn't get together. Well, I won't be long, Herbie. When I come back, we'll go to the market together."

She walked off, hoping to see Willoughby once more, but he had hurried off. He had become quite nervous about the thought of facing his uncle.

Alonzo Hawk hadn't forgotten his nephew. He was asking his secretary, "Has that nephew of mine showed up this morning?"

"Not yet," she answered.

"Then call him wherever he's staying," Hawk commanded. "Tell him to get himself right over here."

"Yes, sir," the secretary replied, "and Mr. Barnsdorf is on the phone for you, sir."

Hawk picked up the phone and said, "Yeah, Barnsdorf, what is it now?"

"Are you ready to dig yet, Hawk?" the voice on the other end said. "My boys are getting itchy."

"No!" Hawk roared. "I'll tell you when to dig!"

"Just thought I'd remind you! I got some high-priced digging equipment and crews sitting around playing gin rummy, waiting for you to make up your mind! It's costing you about eight grand a day."

Hawk could hear the man on the other end laughing after he had mentioned the cost to Hawk. "Stop bothering me, Barnsdorf," Hawk warned. "You'll get an order to dig any moment now."

Then as Hawk slammed down the receiver, he caught sight of his secretary in the doorway. "Well, what is it?" he asked.

"I'm sorry," she said. "I called the motel, but your nephew has checked out."

At that moment, Willoughby had just entered the outer office, but neither Hawk nor his secretary knew the young man was there.

"What do you mean, he checked out?" Hawk exploded with anger. "When? Where to? Who said he could check out? How dare he disappear when he knows I'm worrying myself sick about the situation? I'll tear his chicken-livered gizzard to shreds! I'll stomp him silly! I'll take this letter knife and stab that kid right through his ungrateful breastbone!"

Hawk paused to take in some air, but Willoughby had overheard enough. He tiptoed out of the office to a phone booth down the hall and dug into his pockets for a dime.

"Millicent," Hawk continued, "you know me. Normally, I'm a kindly fun-loving soul. But if someone lets me down, I go bananas!"

Millicent didn't have to agree. The phone

40

rang, and she picked it up and listened. Then she handed it to Hawk. "It's your nephew, sir," she said.

Almost choking with rage, Hawk screamed, "Willoughby! Where are you!"

"Oh, hi, Uncle," Willoughby said cheerfully into the receiver. "I just thought I'd save time and phone you the news."

"The news?" Hawk said, and a look of greed spread over his face. "You got the old fire-ax to sign the papers! Marvelous! Great! Good boy! I knew Hawk blood would tell in the end!"

In the phone booth, Willoughby was making various ship sounds and calling "all ashore" in a heavy Swedish accent.

"What are all those funny sounds?" Hawk asked. "And what news?"

"Oh," Willoughby said. "News I was leaving town. I'm on the ship-to-shore phone. From the deck of a Swedish freighter bound for Helsinki. Uncle? Did you hear me?"

Hawk had heard him. He was in such a rage that he couldn't get a word out.

"Glad you're taking it like this, Uncle," Willoughby continued. "You know you really ought to let Mrs. Steinmetz alone. She doesn't want to leave the firehouse. And that brings up another point. You should leave San Francisco alone too. It's quite beautiful as it is."

Hawk could take no more. His wild terrifying scream almost tore off Willoughby's ear, and he pulled the telephone receiver away from it. The terrifying scream continued at such a high pitch that it shattered the four glass walls of the telephone booth. Willoughby stepped quickly and carefully through the broken shards, turned up his coat collar, and headed for the elevator. He wanted no more of Uncle Alonzo Hawk.

The news had sent Hawk reeling onto his sofa, and his secretary and lawyers had come running to his side.

"It's the same old story," Hawk groaned. "Everyone stabs me in the back — even my own flesh and blood."

"Now don't worry, Mr. Hawk," a lawyer said. "I'm sure you'll feel better in the morning."

Hawk stared hard at the lawyer. "Don't talk like an idiot," he said. "I feel better now. Alonzo Hawk may be betrayed, but he is never defeated. And since none of you pitiful excuses for men have enough muscle to get this feeble old lady off the property, I'll just have to do it myself! The same as I have to do anything important!"

Shaking off helping hands, Hawk pulled himself up and started for his desk. His lawyers followed, mumbling weak protests.

"Shut up!" Hawk told them. "We go to step

number one — harassment! I wrote the book on harassment! First of all, we cut off her water. Then we have the phone turned off. Then we sic the health and building inspectors on her. Next, we steal her dog!"

"She has no dog," a lawyer corrected.

"Ridiculous!" Hawk answered. "A little old lady living in a place like that! Who takes care of her? How does she get around?"

"She has a little car," another lawyer said. "She goes everywhere in it."

"OK, fine," Hawk said. "Some of you go and pick it up."

He led the lawyers to the door, motioning for them to leave. Then he said, "Hold it! You'll blow even a simple assignment like that. The First Team is on the job now. I'll pick it up myself. Follow me!"

Seconds later, Hawk and his lawyers stepped out of the building onto the sidewalk. They headed for Hawk's Rolls-Royce which was parked on his private drive.

After gesturing to his chauffeur, Hawk told the lawyers, "You're probably unaware of it, but I began my fabulous career as a repossessor of motor cars. At the tender age of nineteen, I was the best-known repossessor of cars west of the Mississippi. 'Hot-wire Hawk' they called me."

Then Hawk turned to Maxwell, his chauffeur,

who handed him a fitted case. Opening it, he said, "Observe! One screwdriver. One pair of pliers. One bent piece of wire. Now check your watches. You will see me return with the object of my mission in fifteen minutes or less."

Hawk's obedient lawyers checked their watches, while he got into the passenger compartment of the luxurious car. "OK — move it out!" Hawk said.

Hawk and his lawyers contemplate taking action against interfering Herbie.

SIX

While Maxwell rang the front doorbell of the firehouse, Hawk sat in his Rolls and cheerfully twisted a coat hanger into shape. With it, he planned to open the door of the VW and steal the little car.

"Madame is not at home, sir," Maxwell said, helping Hawk out of the car.

"Thank you, Maxwell," Hawk said. "You may go now. I won't be needing you anymore today."

Quickly and professionally, Hawk set to work. Using the coat hanger, he opened Herbie's door. Then he went around to the rear of the car and started Herbie's engine. Seconds later, Hawk was driving through San Francisco, looking like the happiest man in the world.

"Like riding a bicycle," Hawk said to himself. "Once you learn something when you're young, you never forget it. But even a child of six could steal this one-cylinder hair dryer!"

Hearing the insult, Herbie stopped suddenly. Hawk tried to get the little car rolling again, but Herbie wasn't in any mood to move. He resisted, and crowds of honking cars began to pile up on all sides of Hawk.

With some tricky maneuvering, a police car managed to slip in behind Herbie, and a tough-looking police sergeant stepped alongside Hawk. "OK, buddy," he said, "let's get this thing out of here before I — Oh it's you, Mr. Hawk. What in the world are you doing in this little car?"

"Just shut up and push!" Hawk commanded.

"Certainly, Mr. Hawk," the sergeant said, starting back for his car. Then he turned and said, "One tiny thing. Is the car out of gear, sir?"

"Of course it's out of gear, you nitwit!" Hawk screamed. "Now push!"

Hustling back to his car, the sergeant got in and signaled his driver to push the little VW. The police car inched forward until its front bumper was flush with Herbie's rear bumper. Then the police car's motor revved up. Herbie

47

revved up too and pushed hard backwards.

The police car was hurtled backward into a Yellow Cab, and the Yellow Cab flew backward; one car after another in the long line began to bump each other. Each car's hood flew open.

As the policemen got out of their car, the sergeant asked, "What'd you do that for?"

"I didn't do it," his driver tried to explain. "Hawk did."

The sergeant had an angry crowd on his hands, and he rushed over to the VW. "Are you trying to get tough, Mr. Hawk?" he asked.

"Don't you dare threaten me!" Hawk answered.

Before the sergeant could respond, a police officer with a lot of braids on his uniform appeared in a second police car. The officer got out of his car and spoke quietly to the other officers. While he was talking, the first police car slipped in front of Herbie and ropes were tied from its rear bumper to Herbie's front bumper. The police had decided to tow away the little VW.

The chief officer stepped over to Hawk and said, "Now sit quietly this time, Mr. Hawk. Don't touch the pedals or gears! Understood?"

"I do exactly what I please!" Hawk complained. "Don't order me around! The traffic commissioner will hear of this!"

Sneering at the threat, the officer said, "I *am* the Commissioner!"

"Then what are you doing in that monkey op-eretta outfit?" Hawk asked. "A commissioner would dress in dignified clothes!"

"This is my dress uniform!" the Commis-sioner informed Hawk. "I was going to the cere-monies for 'I Am a Policeman Day'!"

The tow was ready, so the Commissioner walked back to his car and got in.

For a moment, Herbie allowed himself to be towed. Then he resisted, stopping first and then starting to pull the big car backward.

"Don't let him do that to you!" the sergeant told his driver.

The police car dug in and started to pull Her-bie forward again. It was a tug-of-war; both cars burned rubber as a crowd of people cheered first for one and then the other.

Back and forth they went, until the rope broke! Then the police car shot forward and plowed smack into the Commissioner's car. The two police cars jack-knifed and stopped in a nose-to-nose position, resting on their rear wheels.

Herbie didn't wait for the Commissioner's reply. He quickly raced away from the scene, heading for Hawk's meeting place.

There the lawyers were checking their watches. "One minute to go!" one lawyer said. "He'll never make it!"

"When Mr. Hawk says he'll do something,

49

he'll do it," another lawyer responded.

In part, he was right, because the little VW came roaring around the corner almost as soon as the words had spilled out of his mouth. But in part, he was wrong, because Herbie threw open his door and threw Hawk out onto the sidewalk at them.

The lawyers couldn't believe their eyes. They stared in amazement at the outstretched body of their leader. "Don't stand there, you idiots!" Hawk screamed. "Get that car — dead or alive!"

The lawyers raced off in fear of Hawk, while he rested on the sidewalk, still trying to catch his breath.

Suddenly a pair of feet caught his attention and he looked up. It was the police sergeant, and in his hand he held a stack of citations. He handed them to Hawk and put a pen in front of him.

"Just sign a few of these citations, please," the sergeant said. "Compliments of the Commissioner."

SEVEN

"I'm sorry Willoughby's leaving," Nicole thought, as she replaced the telephone receiver.

Grandma Steinmetz had told her what Willoughby planned to tell his uncle, and Nicole realized that she might have misjudged him.

She stepped away from the phone, but she was stopped by the sound of a familiar voice. She stopped to listen.

"I tell you, Mother, you've never seen Uncle Alonzo in such a rage," the voice said. "He's probably having this airport watched right now."

Nicole turned and stared in surprise at a man with a beard and moustache. "Yes, Mother, I know I promised I wouldn't grow a beard when I left home, but you don't understand. It isn't real, Mother."

Nicole knew for certain then. It was Willoughby. She smiled and moved closer to him, but he didn't catch sight of her.

"No, Mother," Willoughby continued, "I am not going back to apologize to Uncle Alonzo. He's a greedy, no-good, thieving..."

Willoughby paused, trying to think of a final word to describe Hawk. From the corner of his eye, he caught sight of a piece of paper on which Nicole had written the word "coyote."

"Coyote," Willoughby said, ending the sentence. "Thank you, miss."

Then Willoughby recognized Nicole and almost leaped away from the phone in shock. Seeing Nicole smile relaxed him. "Nothing's the matter with me, Mother," he said into the phone. "Everything's fine now. Uncle Alonzo used to push me around, and *you* were always telling me what to do. But now I've met this perfectly wonderful girl, and until now I was afraid of her too."

Willoughby saw the sparkle in Nicole's eyes. "This is the turning point of my life, Mother," he said. "I'm not going to be a rabbit anymore! Yes — I knew you would be glad for me! Good-

Nicole stares in surprise as a clumsily disguised Willoughby reassures his mother by long-distance telephone.

bye, Mother, and...yes, I'll write you!"

After putting down the receiver, Willoughby reached for his chin and tore off the false beard and moustache. "Ouch! That hurt," he said.

Nicole gave him a quick kiss and said, "It'll be all right. And now you'd better buy me a cup of coffee, because I think I missed my plane."

While Willoughby and Nicole were looking for a nice quiet place to be alone together, Grandma was moving toward the shopping market in her little VW. She was so busy looking over her shopping list, she didn't notice the three black Lincoln Continentals coming up the hill at her. But Herbie saw them! He skidded sharply to a stop, turned, and raced off in the opposite direction!

"Herbie," Grandma said, not realizing what was happening, "I'm trying to go through my shopping list. Now be careful!"

Herbie hadn't lost the three Continentals. They were racing after him and closing ground. Hawk's lawyers were in each of the cars, and he was in his office, directing them over their car phones.

"Don't wait!" Hawk screamed into his phone. "Go in and smash it!"

"Moving in for the kill now, Mr. Hawk," one lawyer responded.

It seemed as if Herbie was trapped. He had

come to a street overlooking the Bay, and a line of Continentals barred its entrance. A wall of earth to Herbie's side seemed to be blocking any chance for escape.

Herbie gunned his motor and raced forward! Then he swung to the side and ran right up the earthen wall! The lawyers couldn't believe their eyes, but they watched in amazement as the little car raced down the wall behind them, turned a corner, and disappeared from sight.

The Continentals swung into action, and in minutes they were again trailing the little VW through San Francisco's downtown streets.

Herbie led them into a parking building. Then with a burst of speed, he circled the ramps leading to the roof. After racing across the roof, Herbie climbed onto the top of another VW. Then he leaped! And what a leap! He went over the street, far below, and landed on the roof of the building across the way! Fortunately, it was another parking building!

Although the hard landing slightly shook Grandma Steinmetz, she was still too absorbed in reviewing her shopping list to realize what was going on. "Now, Herbie, behave," she murmured gently. "You almost knocked my glasses off!"

Herbie headed down the ramps for the street, and for a few minutes, he had smooth sailing. When Hawk's lawyers spotted him again, he was crossing the sidewalk and entering the Sheraton Palace Hotel. Ready now to believe anything about the little VW, they jumped from their cars and continued the chase on foot.

Herbie rolled through the hotel's main dining room so silently that its occupants never even noticed it. Only a waiter, carrying a huge cake, spotted him going out of the kitchen, and the waiter decided his eyes were playing tricks on him. He turned and started for the dining room. Hawk's lawyers smashed into him, sending the cake flying.

Hawk was fuming. He hadn't been able to get his lawyers on their car phones, and he was telling his secretary what he planned to do with them when he got his hands on them.

It was she who spotted Herbie on the Golden Gate Bridge. "There it is!" She pointed out Hawk's window. "There it is! It's climbing up the side of the Bridge!"

Hawk didn't bother to look. "Come on, Millicent!" he said angrily. "Pull yourself together! Now you're getting hysterical too! Just take a couple of aspirin and lie down!"

Millicent staggered out of the office, holding

Herbie rolls silently through main dining room of the Sheraton-Palace. Inside car a bemused Mrs. Steinmetz ponders shopping list.

her head, and Hawk idly glanced out of the window. Then *he* saw it too! Herbie was chasing his lawyers down the cablewalk of the bridge tower! It was enough for Hawk! He rushed out to get some aspirin!

Sometime later, the little VW pulled up to the firehouse and honked. Nicole came out, followed by Willoughby. "Hi, Grandma," Nicole said. "I was worried when you weren't home. Everything all right?"

"Just wonderful," Mrs. Steinmetz answered, starting to unload her groceries. "Herbie took me for a nice drive on the Bridge."

EIGHT

They needed more broccoli for dinner. Mrs. Steinmetz hadn't planned on feeding three. Nicole and Willoughby volunteered to go for it.

As they were getting into the car, Mrs. Steinmetz whispered to Nicole, "Why don't you drive to the beach afterwards. It's a beautiful day."

"Grandma!" Nicole answered. "Stay out of this! We're just going to get broccoli!"

Mrs. Steinmetz nodded. Then she patted Herbie's hood and whispered, "Herbie, I'm not going to say a word. There's nothing I can do. I can't help it if you have a mind of your own. Can I?"

Herbie got the message. He allowed Nicole to drive him to the grocery, but when Willoughby returned with the broccoli, Herbie took charge. Nicole wrestled with the wheel, but Herbie knew where he wanted to go.

"Grandma put him up to this," Nicole explained to Willoughby.

"Where's he taking us?" Willoughby asked.

"I don't know," she said, smiling, "But I could make a guess."

As they crossed the Golden Gate Bridge into Marin County, Nicole *knew* that Herbie was going to the beach, but she didn't know that they were being followed by Hawk's chauffeur.

"It would appear, sir, that the young lady and gentleman are not immediately returning to the firehouse," the chauffeur reported to Hawk on the car's radiophone.

"OK," Hawk answered from his office. "You see that they don't! Do anything you have to, but keep them away from the firehouse until dark."

Soon Herbie pulled down a steep road to the beach, passing an old camper parked at the top of the bluff.

"It's a put-up job," Nicole said, looking out at the beach, but Willoughby had no idea what she was talking about.

They got out and rested on the sand, while Herbie raced up and down the beach, chasing sea gulls. At the same time, Hawk's chauffeur

Up and down beach a playful Herbie chases sea gulls.

was arranging with the owner of the camper for him to block the road.

"It's very romantic here," Willoughby told Nicole.

Smiling slightly, Nicole said, "I'm sure it's what Grandma had in mind. She always thought the Pacific Ocean was romantic. Goes back to the time Captain Steinmetz proposed to her on the beach near the old Cliff House fifty years ago."

"How do *you* feel?" Willoughby asked.

Nicole studied him for a minute. Then she said, "I haven't made up my mind yet, but I wish I hadn't punched you the first time I met you."

"That's OK," Willoughby answered.

"And the other time it wasn't very ladylike to hit you in the face with that broiled lobster," Nicole added. "You can hit me back if you want to."

"That wasn't exactly what I had in mind," Willoughby said. Then he leaned over and kissed her.

Sand broke the spell. Herbie accidentally kicked it all over them, as he raced by. "Herbie!" Nicole called after the car and looked at her watch. "It's time to be getting back."

By the time Nicole and Willoughby had the

Willoughby finally makes peace with a somewhat chastened Nicole.

sand brushed off themselves, Herbie had moved into position alongside them. Before they got into the car, Nicole kissed Willoughby again.

When they reached the camper, it was clear the road was blocked. "My axle's broken," the camper's owner told Willoughby.

Herbie backed quickly down the road, without waiting for Willoughby to respond. On the beach again, Herbie started a long run out along the jetty toward the sea, while Nicole and Willoughby watched in shocked silence.

Soon the little car dove off the end of the jetty into the sea, and Willoughby held his nose. They were sinking!

Seconds later, the little car rose to the surface and began to motorboat along the surf line. This new style of travel seemed to please Herbie's passengers, until Willoughby looked through the rear window.

"Nicole," he said, showing some signs of fear, "very quietly and very quickly pull your hand back inside the car!"

"Why?" Nicole asked.

"We've got company," he answered, gesturing for her to look out the back window.

Nicole spotted the shark's fin! She gasped

Making a mighty leap from a jetty, Herbie launches himself into Pacific Ocean.

and quickly withdrew her hand from the water. "That's ridiculous," she said. "Why would a shark be following a Volkswagen?"

"Because he thinks we're going to sink," Willoughby answered, shuddering at the thought.

But they didn't sink, and aside from wiping out a surprised surfer, they had a smooth ride to the far shore. The trouble started when they reached the firehouse. Everything was gone, and Mrs. Steinmetz was seated on the stairs, staring sadly into space.

"Who did it?" Nicole asked her.

Without looking at them, Mrs. Steinmetz said, "They came with a big truck. On the truck it said, 'Alonzo Hawk Van and Storage.' "

As Herbie valiantly chugs for home, a shark follows him through the water.

NINE

It didn't take long for the three of them to find Hawk's Van and Storage. But there they were stuck. Willoughby couldn't jimmy open the door.

"Do something," Nicole told him. "We can't hang around here!"

The sound of Herbie revving up interrupted their thoughts. Then they watched as the little car raced forward and crashed through the doors. They smiled at each other and moved into the warehouse.

"Halt!" a voice warned. "You have been detected by electronic surveillance! You are about to be surrounded by agents of the Alonzo Hawk Security Service!"

A look of anger shot across Mrs. Steinmetz's face.

"Touch nothing in this warehouse," the voice continued, "or you will be prosecuted to the full extent of the law!"

"Don't you dare talk to me like that, Mr. Hawk!" Mrs. Steinmetz called out. "I want my things back, and I'm going to get them!"

"I think it's a recording," Willoughby told her.

"I don't care what it is," Mrs. Steinmetz answered.

Willoughby moved forward. "Come on," he said. "Let's find your things before someone gets here!"

They hurried up and down long corridors, looking for Mrs. Steinmetz's furnishings. Finally, Willoughby whispered, "I don't think your things are here."

Before Mrs. Steinmetz could answer, she heard the sound of her orchestrion. Following the music, they found Mrs. Steinmetz's things, including the cable car, piled high behind a curtained enclosure.

"Hold it!" a voice warned them.

Turning, they saw two armed guards rushing at them.

"Get your hands up!" ordered the first guard. "You're the birds who've been breaking in here lately."

Grandma Steinmetz stood her ground. "Don't get fresh with me, young man," she warned.

"Watch out, Smitty!" the first guard told his partner. "She's the ringleader."

"Move it, Grandma, and get those hands up," the second guard said, not noticing Herbie silently backing away.

"I most certainly will not!" Grandma Steinmetz told him. "If you say 'please,' I might consider it."

While Grandma and the guard continued their argument, Herbie ran up a ramp to the second floor and slipped in behind a stack of furniture piled near the edge of the loft. Then he pushed it over the side!

The furniture crashed in the area between the guards and their captives. The force of the crash sent furniture spilling down all over the warehouse. The guards ran for their lives! But they were trapped! They were locked inside a jungle of furniture!

On the other side of the furniture jungle, Willoughby quickly took charge. He, Nicole, and Mrs. Steinmetz loaded all her things onto the cable car. Then Mrs. Steinmetz seated herself in Old 22, and Nicole and Willoughby climbed into Herbie.

It was a tough job for Herbie. He pushed the cable car out of the warehouse and slowly shoved it toward the top of a steep San Francisco hill.

About halfway up the hill, the cable car took on a passenger. A tired old rancher, wearing boots and a cowboy hat climbed aboard.

After settling into a seat, the rancher saw Grandma Steinmetz, and said, "Evening, Mother. Ain't you a bit old to be a stewardess? Things sure have changed since the day I come to visit this town."

The rancher was fast asleep before Mrs. Steinmetz could answer him.

Meanwhile, Nicole sensed some of the danger they would be facing at the top of the hill. Turning to Willoughby, she said, "Better stop Herbie at the top of the hill. We need to figure out what happens going down the other side."

"I'd better get a chunk of rope and tie us all together nice and snug," Willoughby suggested, stopping Herbie and getting out.

He found rope and tied up some of the furniture on the car. Then he started to tie Herbie to the cable car, but a line of cars coming up the hill caught his eye. He looked carefully. Then he said, almost as if to himself, "Look out! It looks like Uncle!"

The threatening line of cars angered Herbie. With a snarling roar, he started backward down the hill toward the oncoming cars. Inside the little car, Nicole tried the brakes and said, "No, Herbie! Don't do it!"

Mr. Judson is glad to be off his feet and sitting on runaway cable car. Nevertheless he wonders what Mrs. Steinmetz is knitting, and why.

Herbie veered off into an alley, while Hawk, in his lead car, screamed to the driver, "Get it! Get it!"

Coming out of the alley with Hawk's car in hot pursuit, Herbie saw the street ahead was blocked by two of Hawk's security cars.

In desperation, Nicole said, "We've either got to pray or fly!"

And fly they did. Using an upset pretzel wagon as a ramp, Herbie lifted off and sailed right over Hawk's security cars!

Following Herbie up the makeshift ramp, Hawk's driver got his car off the ground, but it was too heavy. Nosing down, it crashed into the line of cars.

Willoughby cheered the events. But then he realized the cable car was gone! He turned and saw it rolling free down the hill. Shouting, he ran off after it.

When Herbie caught up with Willoughby, the cable car was still running loose. On the run, Willoughby leaped into the little VW through the sunroof.

"Grandma'll get hurt," Nicole complained. "How come you let the cable car get away?"

"Never mind," Willoughby said anxiously. "Just hurry up!"

Maybe Grandma *was* going to be hurt, but she

wasn't thinking about it. The rancher had waked up, and they were deep into a nice conversation, one that even hinted of romance. Neither of them noticed they were racing down an extremely steep hill, heading for the cold waters of San Francisco harbor.

With a burst of speed, Herbie got alongside the runaway cable car. Willoughby, quickly climbing through the sunroof, prepared to jump. When it seemed the right time, he leaped!

And what a leap! It was very nearly perfect. All Nicole had to do was lean out and plant his dangling legs firmly on the cable car. From there he was on his own, and he struggled over the piled-up furniture, dived for the hand brake, and pulled it back as hard as he could. Sparks flew from the rear of the car as it came to a stop! Nicole sighed. The cable car's front wheels were dangling over the water.

"Well, here's where I get off," the rancher told Mrs. Steinmetz. "And thanks for the ride, little lady. I sure hope to be seeing you again soon."

Exhausted from the chase, Nicole and Willoughby limped up to Grandma Steinmetz. "Are you all right?" Nicole asked.

"Of course," Grandma said. "I've just met the most interesting man. But I'll tell you all about him after we get home.

TEN

Before leaving for the airport next day, Nicole said to Willoughby, "I know Grandma, and I think she's up to something."

"Don't worry," Willoughby answered. "I'll keep her out of mischief."

Nicole kissed Willoughby. "Be sure you do," she said warmly. "Or I may get tough again!"

After watching Nicole's bus disappear down the street, Willoughby turned and saw Mrs. Steinmetz standing on the sidewalk with her hat on. "Where are you going?" he asked, suspiciously.

Without hesitation, Grandma answered, "To

see Mr. Hawk." Then she started for the car.

"Do you mind if I come with you?" Willoughby said, following her to the driver's side of the car.

"What for?" Mrs. Steinmetz replied. "To stop me from seeing your uncle?"

"No, but I'd like to keep an eye on you. I think Nicole would prefer it," Willoughby said, closing the door for her and moving around to the other side of the car.

Before he reached the passenger side, Herbie shot away from the curb. Willoughby started after the car, calling to Grandma to wait for him. Then he stopped. He realized he wasn't going to catch Herbie, as long as Herbie didn't want to be caught.

Alonzo Hawk didn't need a visit from Mrs. Steinmetz. In fact, he felt almost beaten by the old woman. Sitting at his desk, he was thinking hard about the problem. Finally, a sinister smile crossed his face. "Millicent, go out there and look up Fred Loostgarten," he told his secretary. "He used to be with our wrecking company before I fired him. I heard he started some sort of little outfit of his own."

"Yes, sir," Millicent said, hurrying outside to do what she had been told.

Hawk sat back and closed his eyes. A peaceful smile came over his face. It would have left had he been aware of the events taking place twenty-eight stories below him.

After reaching the Hawk Building, Grandma Steinmetz looked around. Her eyes zeroed in on a window-washing rig, and she walked over to the operator who had just switched off the console and attached the key to his belt. "Excuse me, young man," she said. "Can you tell me where Mr. Hawk's office is?"

"Yes, ma'am," the operator answered. "The old buzzard hangs out twenty-eight stories up and six windows to the left. You can't miss it."

Moving closer to the operator, Grandma Steinmetz said, "Once more, please. I don't hear very well on this side."

"Twenty-eighth floor!" the operator said, getting very close to Mrs. Steinmetz. "You can't miss it."

As he turned away, Grandma slipped the console key from his belt. "Thank you very much!" she said.

She watched the operator walk off. Then Herbie rolled onto the window-washing rig, and Grandma put the key into the console. She turned it and pressed the button marked "UP."

Just as the rig started its upward journey, Willoughby leaped from a taxicab and called, "No! Grandma, stop!"

He raced for the rig and managed to get his

77

hands on the edge of the platform. The platform continued its upward movement, while Grandma listened to Herbie's radio, unaware that Willoughby was barely hanging from the platform's edge.

As the rig went higher and higher up the side of the building, Grandma became annoyed at a commercial and switched off the radio. Then Willoughby's frantic calls for help reached her ear. Leaning out of the car window and looking around, she saw Willoughby's fingers on the edge of the platform. "There you are!" she said smiling. "Just a moment! I'm coming!"

"No! No!" Willoughby screamed. "Stay where you are! Just take us down!"

"Of course," Grandma Steinmetz said, moving to the platform's edge. "But first you must promise to let me see Mr. Hawk!"

"Anything!" Willoughby pleaded. "I'll do anything you say!"

"Very good!" Grandma said, offering him a hand. "Now come on up here. You know, you shouldn't take such chances."

Inside the building, Hawk was smiling. He had gotten Fred Loostgarten on the phone and he had decided that Loostgarten was the man he needed. "So I said to myself, I must find a job for my old friend Loostgarten, and here it is," he said into the receiver. "You know that crummy firehouse where I'm going to build Hawk Plaza? Well, I want you to take your wrecking ball and smash it. That's right! I want nothing left but a grease spot!"

Hawk's look of pleasure changed to anger as he listened to Loostgarten's response. "What permit?" Hawk roared. "I won't have the permit until tomorrow. But don't argue with me, Loostgarten, that's how you got in trouble last time! The job has to be done tonight. We start digging in the morning. It's three thousand now, and three thousand more when you've done the job."

Again Hawk listened. Then he said quickly, before hanging up the phone, "Thanks, buddy boy. I knew I could count on you."

If Hawk hadn't been so excited about the deal he had just made, he might've heard the window-washing rig come to a stop outside his open windows. But he was too busy talking through the intercom to his secretary. "I've just made a deal with Loostgarten," he said. "Tonight he's going to smash that crummy old firehouse to matchwood. It'll certainly teach that old battle-ax a lesson."

Grandma Steinmetz had heard enough. Before Willoughby could stop her, she hit the window-washing console's operating lever. A huge wave of sudsy water blasted into the office, and for a moment Hawk went under.

"No, no!" Willoughby begged. "He won't like that!"

"I don't care what he doesn't like," Grandma said, shooting another blast of suds at Hawk. "Take that, Mr. Hawk!"

Willoughby staggered out of the car and tried to work his way through the soap and water to the console's controls. "Don't worry, Uncle!" he called. "Everything's under control!"

"Sure it is!" Hawk called back angrily. Then he picked up an ashtray and heaved it in Willoughby's direction. It missed Willoughby and banged off Herbie's side.

"Now you've done it, Mr. Hawk!" Grandma warned. "I'm afraid you've made Herbie very angry!"

She was right. First, Herbie did a wheelie! Then he charged off the rig, across the windowsill, and into Hawk's office!

Terrified, Hawk turned and ran for his life!

Herbie shot through the suds and chased Hawk around a conference table. Willoughby ran after the little VW, hoping to stop it, but he slipped on some suds and fell.

"All right, Herbie," Grandma Steinmetz pleaded. "We've had our fun. That's quite enough!"

Herbie has heard enough. Charging off the window-washing rig and through the window he takes off after Alonzo Hawk in a wave of white suds.

Herbie roared forward, searching for Hawk who had disappeared again under the sea of foam. Then Herbie skidded into a pedestal. The statue on it dropped, landing on Hawk's head just emerging from the suds.

"Uncle!" Willoughby said, running over to the groggy Hawk. "Now's a good time to explain."

The sight of Willoughby awakened Hawk. He reached for his nephew's throat! Before he could get his hands around Willoughby's neck, Herbie rushed him! Crawling for his life, Hawk managed to get behind his private bar just before Herbie crashed into it. Then Hawk got up, ran for the door, and threw it open!

Hawk's lawyers and his secretary were surprised to see him slide into the room. They were even more surprised to see him get to his feet and run out into the main corridor. But they were amazed at the sight of the VW chasing him into the corridor! And then came Willoughby in pursuit of the little car!

Finally Willoughby reached the car and got inside. Hawk had climbed out a window and onto the building's ledge, into safety, he thought!

Herbie shot onto the ledge! "Stop him!" Wil-

Thoroughly coated with detergent suds and tired of being chased around his office by Herbie, Hawk has just about had it.

loughby screamed, looking over the side to the street far below.

"There's one thing Herbie's afraid of," Grandma Steinmetz said softly to herself. Then she called, "Stop, Herbie! Don't make me do it!"

"Please do it!" Willoughby begged.

Hawk had reached the end of the ledge. It was the street — or the VW!

"I should certainly hate to call Mr. Honest Al, the Used Car Man," Grandma said, winking at Willoughby. "I wouldn't want him to come by and pick up my sweet little car! But if Herbie can't behave..."

Herbie stopped short! Then he started to inch his way backward.

"I wouldn't do it," Grandma whispered to Willoughby. "And I don't think Herbie believes it either. But it always works!"

Feeling somewhat safe for the moment, Hawk called, "I'll get you for this, Willoughby! I will, if it's the last thing I do! And I'll get that nutty old lady too!"

After being lowered down the side of the building in the window-washing rig, Herbie and his passengers headed for home. "By the way," Grandma said, "did we get the name of the gentleman who thinks he's going to knock down my firehouse?"

Willoughby didn't remember. He really hadn't recovered completely from the ride around the building's ledge.

Fortunately, Grandma remembered. "It was a Mr. Loostgarten at the Loostgarten Wrecking Company," she said cheerfully. "Well, I'll just write his name down. We're going to need Mr. Loostgarten."

ELEVEN

Nicole didn't appreciate what had happened at Hawk's building, and she blamed Willoughby for not taking care of Grandma Steinmetz. She didn't want to hear his explanation. All she wanted was Hawk's home address. With it, they could handle Loostgarten. But the address wasn't listed in the phone book, and his office wouldn't provide it. It looked as if they weren't going to be able to put Grandma's plan into operation.

Finally Willoughby said, "I don't care how angry you are. I'm going to say something."

"Go ahead," Nicole answered, still annoyed with him.

"I've sent Uncle Alonzo a card every Christmas since I was seven years old," Willoughby said, handing her a small address book. "Here's his address."

For a moment, Nicole didn't understand why he hadn't spoken sooner. Then she realized that she had kept him from speaking. "You are wonderful!" she said, pulling him to her and kissing him.

After that, it was time for practice, and Willoughby ran over his voice impersonation of Alonzo Hawk while Nicole and Grandma listened. Then Nicole dialed Loostgarten's number and handed the receiver to Willoughby.

"This is Alonzo Hawk," Willoughby told Loostgarten.

"Oh, yes, Mr. Hawk," Loostgarten answered. "What can I do for you now?"

"Loostgarten, there's a change of plans," Willoughby told him. "I don't want you to knock down that firehouse tonight. Instead I want you to knock down 343 Oleander Heights."

Willoughby paused, smiling at Nicole. Then he said, "It's 343 Oleander Heights. Write it down! I don't want to see you lose your place in the wrecking business, so make sure you do a good job!"

Willoughby hung up the phone, and Nicole threw her arms around his neck. "Perfect," she said. "Just perfect!"

Hawk couldn't fall asleep. He was worried about the firehouse. He hoped by morning it would be gone forever. Finally, counting sheep, he dozed off. The night around him was silent.

The sheep in Hawk's dream turned into Volkswagens. They had sharp teeth, and they were jumping the fence and coming after him. Then his dream changed.

Hawk was crouched like King Kong on top of the Empire State Building. Flying Volkswagens were circling him and squirting oil in his face. He tried to wipe his face and lost his grip on the building. He was falling through the air, faster and faster. Then the phone rang. Hawk came out of his dream.

"What is it?" he said into the receiver.

"This is Loostgarten," the voice on the other end said. "I'm sorry to bother you at this time of night, Mr. Hawk, but a guy in my job can't afford to make mistakes."

"What are you talking about?" Hawk said, not yet fully awake.

"The address you gave me over the phone— 343 Oleander Heights," Loostgarten said. "You sure that's the right address?"

"Of course I'm sure, you idiot! I know it as well as I know my own address."

Sheep in Hawk's troubled sleep have turned into Volkswagens with sharp teeth.

Hawk slammed down the receiver. He started to lie down again. Then he jumped up and screamed, "Wait a minute! It *is* my own address!"

Before Hawk could get out another word, a giant wrecking ball slammed into the side of his house. Hawk ran for the window, but it was too late! The ball hit again! This time, half the bedroom wall collapsed!

The house was almost completely demolished whe Loostgarten spotted Hawk. He was picking up a two-by-four to use on the wrecker. Loostgarten didn't wait to explain. He jumped out of the cab of his machine and ran down the street. Something had gone wrong, but Hawk didn't seem in the mood for any explanations.

Hawk gave chase, while the last remaining bits and pieces of his home crumbled to the ground.

TWELVE

Joy filled the firehouse the next morning. The morning newspaper headline told it all. Hawk had given up. He was calling an end to his giant building project.

"We beat him!" Grandma Steinmetz said.

"I knew he'd cave in!" Nicole added. "He just couldn't stand the heat!"

The sound of the phone interrupted their celebration. Grandma picked up the receiver and smiled. It was Hawk.

"Now that it's all over," he said, "I just wanted to phone you and say how much I admire you in your plucky fight to save that sweet little firehouse!"

"That's very generous of you," Grandma answered.

"I had a change of heart," Hawk explained. "You see, an accident happened to my little house. It brought home to me how terrible it is to lose something you love."

"Oh! What happened?" Grandma asked innocently.

"Well, a very confused man came along and smashed it to rubble," Hawk explained. "But it did serve one useful purpose. It made me realize I could never tear down any more of San Francisco's beautiful old buildings. So don't worry that dear old gray head anymore. I may even drop by for a cup of tea one of these days, but good-bye for now, Mrs. Steinmetz."

The three began to rejoice.

While Grandma, Nicole, and Willoughby rejoiced, Hawk had other plans. He had just begun to fight.

"I'm glad you've decided to give up Hawk Plaza," his lawyer told him.

"What kind of lawyer are you?" Hawk asked. "You've been fooled like everyone else by that phony news story."

"But you can't go back on it," the lawyer said.

"Can't I?" Hawk replied, looking at the

three lawyers. "In case you amateurs don't recognize it, it is total war now! I'm going to be finishing off the firehouse — once and for all!"

Hawk had guessed right. In the evening, Nicole and Willoughby had gone to the restaurant on the wharf to celebrate. There they were supposed to meet Grandma, and Grandma would have come, except she had a visitor. Mr. Judson, the rancher she had met on her cable car ride, had come to call. Keeping the news about her visitor to herself, Grandma had called the restaurant and told Nicole to celebrate without her. Then she turned her attention back to Mr. Judson.

"You know, I never seen a fine-looking woman like yourself who took such an interest in cows!" Judson told her.

"It's perfectly natural, Mr. Judson," Grandma answered. "A cow is a useful, as well as an extremely decorative animal!"

Judson's eyes lit up, but before he could respond, a low rumbling sound caught their attention. Grandma climbed out of her seat, got on her knees, and pressed her ear to the floor.

"Why in tarnation are you doing that?" Judson asked.

"I'm not sure," Grandma said. "I think I saw it once in a movie."

The walls began to shake. Then cracks appeared in the ceiling and plaster fell! Herbie blew a warning on his horn! Captain Steinmetz's picture dropped, and the glass over it shattered!

Grandma picked up the picture and stared at it. "Just let me get my hands on the brute responsible for this!" she said.

"Horsewhippin's too good for him," Judson added.

The two of them went to the door, and through the mist, they could see an army of earth movers, tractors, steam shovels, and garbage trucks moving toward them. Sitting in a jeep and leading the oncoming army was Alonzo Hawk!

"Look out!" Grandma said, pushing Judson back into the firehouse. "It's Mr. Hawk!"

Hearing Hawk's name, Herbie came to life! His engine snorted, and he ripped forward out of his stall, heading for the front door.

"Herbie, don't you dare!" Grandma called.

But it was too late! Herbie burst through the double doors and raced at the oncoming jeep. Hawk leaped out of the jeep and ran for cover behind it, but to his surprise the VW just shot by and disappeared into the mist and darkness.

"Herbie must have gone for help!" Grandma

Hawk, leading an army of earth movers, tractors, and steam shovels, is startled to see Herbie leaping through firehouse door and heading for him.

told Judson, as the two of them quickly barricaded the front door.

"I just hope he makes it through to the fort!" Judson said. "I figure we must be cut off or something!"

Hawk's voice coming through a bullhorn said, "OK, Steinmetz, we know you're in there! We've got you surrounded! You got ten minutes to get your things together and get out! Then I grind this dump into powder!"

While Grandma and Judson were looking nervously at each other and wondering what was going to happen, Nicole and Willoughby were looking romantically at each other. They were wondering if they should leave, since they were done eating. Herbie's frantic honking from outside decided for them.

When they reached the street, Herbie threw both his doors open. Nicole and Willoughby jumped in.

"I smell trouble," Nicole said, as Herbie slammed his doors shut.

Then Herbie did a wheelie and charged off! He raced through the seats of San Francisco, sounding his horn like a bugle call to battle!

A parked Volkswagen heard the call. His lights came on. Then his motor. In seconds he was in line behind Herbie.

Turning, Nicole saw the VW following them and said, "We just picked up a friend."

As Herbie continued through the streets, Volkswagens joined him, coming from all directions. They raced out of garages! They raced off of used car lots! They answered the call! Herbie was gathering his own army!

"Three minutes to go, Steinmetz!" Hawk called through his bullhorn, not knowing that trouble for him was on its way.

THIRTEEN

Grandma and Judson used their last three minutes in preparation for the battle. First, they climbed to the tower, and Grandma ran up the flag of San Francisco's "Hook and Ladder 29." Then when they heard Hawk call, "Gentlemen, start your engines," they slid down the brass pole and readied their weapons.

Judson smashed out the window in front with a fire-ax, and Grandma took down Captain Steinmetz's fire hat. Handing it to Judson, she said, "I think Captain Steinmetz would have liked you to wear this."

Judson tossed off his Stetson and put on the chief's hat. "Be mighty proud to, little lady," he said. "Mighty proud."

Then while Grandma readied herself at the water valve lever, Judson aimed the nozzle of the fire hose through the window at the army advancing toward them. When the first steam shovel came into sight, Judson called, "Fire!"

The burst of water knocked the driver out onto the ground, and he started to run. "Fire again!" Judson called, taking careful aim.

The second burst sent the running man sprawling on the seat of his pants, and Judson chalked up a score on the firehouse blackboard.

"Fine shooting, Mr. Judson!" Grandma said.

Nodding proudly, Judson said, "I allow that one won't trouble us for a while"

Next, Hawk sent a bulldozer forward. But again Judson scored a direct hit, sending the bulldozer's driver sailing out of his seat. Getting overconfident, Judson called, "Keep up the pressure, ma'am! We've got the devils on the run!"

It was the wrong order, but Grandma dutifully threw the lever to full pressure. It was too much for the old fire hose. It burst, and the water from it slammed Judson against the wall. Grandma quickly shut down the water and rushed to Judson's side. "Are you all right?" she asked.

"Don't worry about me, ma'am," he said courageously. "We have other worries. We're plumb out of ammunition!"

Hawk must have sensed their troubles. "We go in together this time!" he told his forces, readying them for a mass attack.

He raised his hand to signal forward motion. Then he paused, catching some strange noise in the distance. His eyes searched the mist. Terror came into his eyes! He saw it — an army of Volkswagens coming directly at him. "Drive!" he screamed at his chauffeur. "Drive for your life!"

With Hawk in the lead, the power shovels, bulldozers, and garbage trucks joined in the retreat. The Volkswagens, led by Herbie, pursued.

Finally, Willoughby said, "All right, Herbie, that's enough now."

"Think you're going to make him stop?" Nicole asked. "Fat chance!"

"Herbie," Willoughby warned, "if you don't stop, you won't be invited to our wedding!"

Herbie skidded to a stop, and his army did the same. The battle was over. Herbie's army had won!

Hawk knew he was the loser, but he didn't know that he was out of danger. His jeep had

"Fine shooting, Mr. Judson." Mrs. Steinmetz encourages retired rancher who is using fire hose to repel Hawk and his invaders.

been wrecked, and he was on foot, running frantically downhill on a San Francisco street. As he turned a corner, he stepped right into the path of a shiny new police car. The car swerved and smashed into a pole.

The police commissioner got out of the wrecked car. "Oh, it's you again, Mr. Hawk," he said. He was angry.

Hawk ran over to the Commissioner and pulled at his sleeve. "Help me!" he begged. "They're after me!"

"What's after you?" the Commissioner asked.

"The little cars!" Hawk said, hysterically. "Hundreds of them! Can't you see them, you idiot!"

The Commissioner could see nothing. Herbie's army had disbanded, and each car had returned to its home. Signaling to his assistant, the Commissioner said, "I wonder if you'd mind coming to my place of business, Mr. Hawk."

Then the two men grabbed Hawk's arms and led him to the police car. It was the end of a long sad day for Mr. Hawk, and the end of a long happy day for Herbie and the people he loved.

They held the wedding in the firehouse. It was a nice day, and Nicole and Willoughby were

Up the street, an army of Volkswagens, Herbie at its head, makes a determined charge for Alonzo Hawk.

very happy. When they rolled out of the fire-house in Herbie, they were surprised to see that Herbie's friends — two rows of Volkswagens — had formed an arch for them to pass under. They kissed, and Herbie drove them off on their honeymoon. To where? Well, only Herbie had the answer to that!

After wedding ceremony, two rows of Volkswagens form honor guard for Nicole, Willoughby, and Herbie.

C.M.K.